QUEST®

THORON
THE LIVING STORM

BY ADAM BLADE

ORCHARD

VAREEN

THE ICE
CASTLE

THE ICY PLAINS

FREESHOR

CITY OF
JENGTOR

WELCOME TO

Collect the special coins in this book. You will earn one gold coin for every chapter you read.

Once you have finished all the chapters, find out what to do with your gold coins at the back of the book.

With special thanks to J.N. Richards

To Elom Baka, a hero in the making

www.beastquest.co.uk

ORCHARD BOOKS

First published in Great Britain in 2016 by The Watts Publishing Group

1 3 5 7 9 10 8 6 4 2

Text © 2016 Beast Quest Limited.
Cover illustrations by Steve Sims © Beast Quest Limited 2016
Inside illustrations by Raúl Horacio Vila (Beehive Illustration) © Beast Quest Limited 2016

Beast Quest is a registered trademark of Beast Quest Limited
Series created by Beast Quest Limited, London

A CIP catalogue record for this book is available from the British Library.

ISBN 978 1 40834 080 6

Printed in Great Britain

The paper and board used in this book are made from wood from responsible sources

Orchard Books
An imprint of Hachette Children's Group
Part of The Watts Publishing Group Limited
Carmelite House, 50 Victoria Embankment, London EC4Y 0DZ

An Hachette UK Company
www.hachette.co.uk
www.hachettechildrens.co.uk

GWILDOR
BORDERLANDS

MUDDY LAKE

MANGROVE
SWAMP

DUNES

DESERT

TAL

CONTENTS

Do you know the worst thing about so-called heroes? They just don't give up.

Well, villains can be just as stubborn... That pesky boy, Tom, and his lackey, Elenna, may have thwarted our siege of Jengtor, but the battle is not over. There are other prizes to be found throughout my kingdom!

In Gwildor's borderlands lie the four pieces of the Broken Star, a legendary "gift" that fell from the sky many, many years ago. Each piece gives its holder immense power, and whoever brings all four pieces together will be undefeatable!

To obtain each piece, one must find a way past the Beasts which guard them. Kensa and I have tricks up our sleeves – and a head-start on our enemies. With the star in our hands, no one will stop us from reclaiming Gwildor.

And then? Avantia!

Your future ruler,

Emperor Jeng

RACE TO THE BORDERLANDS

Tom could sense the fear spreading through the Freeshor tribespeople. Men, women and children stood with shoulders hunched as if they could make themselves smaller and disappear into the icy landscape.

"Nowhere is safe," Dylar, the tribe's leader murmured, pulling his thick furs tighter around his body. "Not while Emperor Jeng and that witch Kensa are on the loose."

"Then they must be stopped!" another tribesman said.

A young woman gave a bitter laugh. "They have magic on their side and we have nothing." Her younger siblings clung to her skirts. "It's impossible."

"Nothing is impossible." Tom strode into the centre of the tribespeople, his gaze sweeping over their worried faces. "I will stop them. I promise."

An older tribesman, bent double with age, stepped forward. "How?" he asked, his hand clenched on the walking stick he held.

Tom's fingers went to the pouch hanging from his belt and released the white shard that he'd won on his last Quest. He held it up for all the tribespeople to see. "I proved

myself in combat and won this from Gryph the Arctic Falcon," he said. "This fragment of the Broken Star has the power to summon freezing air. Kensa and Jeng wanted it to strengthen their Dark Magic, but I stopped them." He placed the shard back in its pouch. "There are three more shards to find, but I will stop the emperor and witch from getting them." His hand dropped to the hilt of his sword. "By the time my Quest is finished, the witch and the treacherous emperor will pose no threat to the Freeshor people."

There were cheers from the tribespeople and Elenna smiled at him proudly, coming to stand at his side.

She didn't need to say it, but Tom knew that she would be with him on every step of this Quest. They both understood how powerful the shards were. If Kensa and Jeng got even one of the star fragments then the whole kingdom would be doomed.

As the tribe's cheers began to quieten, Dylar strode forward. "Tell me where you're both heading now. It would be my honour to help you."

"Koldo the Artic Warrior told us that we must go north-west," Tom explained. "To a place called Vareen."

Dylar grimaced. "Vareen is in the borderlands. I've never been there, but I've heard it is a barren, desolate place from which travellers rarely return."

"Great," Elenna murmured, an eyebrow arched. "We love Quests with an easy start."

Dylar gave a smile of approval. "You are clearly brave, but you'll still need transportation. The borderlands are many leagues from here." He put two fingers in his mouth and gave a sharp whistle.

Almost immediately, a tribesperson arrived with a wooden sledge by his side. The sledge was pulled by four muscular Gwildorian huskies. Their fur was a russet colour, the same shade of a sunset in Avantia, and their eyes were an emerald green.

"They're beautiful." Elenna knelt

down and stroked each huskie in
turn. Tom could tell she was missing
Silver, her pet wolf.

"Beautiful, but unpredictable,"

Dylar warned. "Still, they will get you to Vareen."

Tom shook his head in protest. "Your offer is very kind. But it would not be fair to leave the dogs on the edge of this new territory while Elenna and I continue our Quest."

"Gwildorian huskies have an amazing sense of direction," Dylar reassured him. "They always find their way home." He shook Tom's hand. "Good luck. My kingdom's future relies on you."

Tom nodded once and then climbed up onto the sledge next to Elenna.

Let the Quest begin, he thought to himself.

They set off, moving northwards

through the icy fields. The blades
of grass were frozen solid and they
crackled and snapped underfoot as
the Gwildorian huskies raced across
the landscape.

The sledge skimmed swiftly across
the plains and Tom's hands tightened
on the reins. He told himself that
it was to control the direction of
the huskies and not because he was
scared of the breakneck speed they
were going. He turned and saw that
Elenna was holding the reins just
as tightly as him. Her cheeks were
red from the wind that lashed them,
and she was concentrating hard on
keeping her balance as they turned a
sharp corner.

Her eyes suddenly widened and Tom whipped round to look up ahead. They were hurtling towards a vast, frozen lake!

"The ice!" Elenna yelled over the wind that was howling past them. "What if it doesn't take our weight?"

Tom yanked on the reins, urging the huskies to stop at the edge of the lake, but they paid him no attention. They leapt straight onto the ice and skidded forwards with yelps of excitement. Beneath their barks, Tom heard the ice of the frozen lake creak in protest as it got used to the weight of the sledge. But it held.

The huskies surged forward and their yelps faded as they focused

on the route ahead. That's when Tom
heard it...

A cracking noise that could mean
only one thing.

The ice is giving way.

Tom looked over his shoulder. A web

of tiny fractures was stretching
towards them.

He snapped the reins. "Go!" he
cried, hoping the huskies would

obey his command this time. "Faster. Go faster!"

The dogs gave a howl of determination and somehow found even more speed. Their strides lengthened, muscles bunching up beneath sleek fur. They charged across the ice and the curving bank at the other side of the lake was now in sight.

Tom checked over his shoulder again. The cracks were still following close behind them but the huskies were faster. "We're going to make—"

Tom broke off as he felt Elenna grip his forearm. She pointed straight ahead. "Look!"

Tom did, and felt the air leave his lungs. The bank of the lake did not lead to safe ground like he'd hoped. It swept upwards and then out to a yawning crevasse.

We're heading to the edge, Tom thought. *And there's nothing I can do to stop it.*

THE VALLEY

"What are we going to do?" Elenna shouted.

Tom scanned the land ahead. The ground would soon drop away and become just air. Even if he used the power of his breastplate, he knew the dogs had gained far too much momentum for him to be able to stop them before the crevasse – they'd just plunge over the edge. There was only one thing for it...

"We jump," he said. "And we hope!"

The huskies took the crevasse

at a leap. Tom's eyes stung as they hurtled forwards and he could feel the force of the leap pushing his cheeks back until they ached.

The drop below seemed endless, but the huskies were moving as if they'd been born to do this. Their bodies arched perfectly and cut through the air.

The sledge landed on the other side of the chasm with a crash that almost threw Tom and Elenna clear. Gritting his teeth, Tom held on tight to the side of the sledge as it clattered over a rocky path that looked very different from the icy terrain they had left behind on the other side of the canyon. He leaned back, harnessing the power from his golden breastplate to try and bring the huskies to a stop.

Eventually, the dogs slowed, and then became still.

Tom turned to Elenna. She was kneeling, holding her shoulder. "Are you all right?" he asked.

Elenna grimaced, but nodded. "I'm much better now that we're on solid ground. The huskies did a great job." She clambered down and patted the dogs.

Tom climbed down as well and looked around at the new terrain. They had arrived in Vareen, he was sure of it. It was just as bleak and inhospitable as Dylar had said. The land stretching before them was mostly made up of rocky valleys lined with ragged pillars that stood like broken statues. There were no signs of life, no signs of any settlements and Tom wondered if Jeng and Kensa had really been brave enough to venture this deep into the borderlands.

Elenna shivered. "Doesn't this place remind you of the Forbidden Land in Avantia?"

Tom shuddered at the memory. "Yes, but at least we don't have Ghost Beasts to worry about here."

Elenna shrugged. "Instead, we just have incredibly powerful Beasts who don't trust humans!"

Tom sighed. "Nonetheless, it's our Quest. The next Beast is out there. The sooner we find it, the sooner we'll prove our worth in combat and win the second fragment of the Broken Star."

Tom and Elenna climbed back

into the sledge, and the huskies set off again, gingerly picking their way along a path that sloped upwards. It looked as cracked and unstable as the ice they had just crossed and the dogs gave low whines of protest. As the huskies weaved their

way through the pillars, Tom heard Elenna gasp.

"What is it?" he asked, his hand going to his sword.

His friend shook her head and looked embarrassed. "It's stupid. For a moment I thought that one of those columns was Koldo. You know how he looks like a living statue. I guess it was just wishful thinking."

Tom smiled as they reached the top of the slope and onto a flat bit of land still studded with stalagmites. "I wish he could be here too, Elenna. It's strange to know we have no Beast friends to call on in the borderlands now we have left Freeshor and—" He broke off as a terrifying rumble shook the air. The sledge lurched to one side, just missing one of the pillars as the huskies gave panicked whines.

All around him, Tom could see the towering rocks shuddering as deep cracks appeared in their bases.

"Be careful," Tom cried. "The pillars are going to collapse!"

With one fluid movement, Tom freed his sword and severed the reins of the sledge. The released huskies darted clear as the rocks thundered downwards one after another.

"We need to move," Tom shouted as he and Elenna tumbled out of the sledge, and straight into the

path of another toppling pillar. Tom
shoved Elenna clear, but the weight
of the rock threw him onto his back.
Gritting his teeth, he kicked

upwards and balanced the pillar for a moment with his feet. The muscles in his calves screamed in protest but he managed to summon enough strength to thrust it off. But Tom knew this was a battle he would not win.

The column of rock kept on falling, crashing onto him. He tried to shield his head, but something hard struck him on the temple and everything went black.

BURIED!

Tom blinked in the darkness. He didn't know how long he had been unconscious. His chest felt tight from the weight of the rocks and the pain of it made him gasp for breath. He tried to concentrate on something other than the agony and called on the power of his golden breastplate. He felt strength flow into his body for an instant and he managed to move it just enough so that the rocks did not crush him.

Tom's head was pounding and he could feel blood trickling down his face. The darkness was coming again and he didn't have the strength to fight it any more.

His world was strangely quiet except for the pounding of his heartbeat in his ears. Tom blinked his way back to consciousness once again. The little light that had managed to seep its way in between the rocks that imprisoned him made his aching head hurt even more.

"Elenna," he called. His mouth was so dry her name came out as a rasp.

She did not respond.

Where is she? Tom wondered. *Is she all right? Is she alive?* He pushed the thought away. Elenna was safe. She had to be.

Nearby, Tom could hear the sound of the huskies' barking and the

clatter of rocks. *They're trying to dig me free,* he thought.

The little slivers of light that leaked between the stones were gathering strength and Tom realised that the huskies were making good progress in freeing him. Then he heard a furious series of barks that quickly turned to frightened-sounding whines...

And then the scramble of paws as the huskies scurried away.

Something was wrong. Tom knew there was no way that the brave, loyal huskies would leave him like this. Unless someone – or something – had scared them off.

Using all the power in his golden

breastplate, he shifted his body once more and tried to slip free of the rock's weight. But every part of him was heavy with tiredness – he couldn't move.

"Your plan worked perfectly," Tom heard a horribly familiar voice say from somewhere close by. *Jeng!* "Do you think the little worm is dead?"

"We can only hope," replied a woman's voice. Kensa. "It will be so much easier to get the white shard from his pocket if he's a corpse."

So the falling pillars were a trap, Tom thought. *And now Jeng and Kensa have scared the huskies away as well.* He clenched his fists. *But I'm no corpse. And our enemies will*

*not take the shard I fought so hard
to win.*

He closed his eyes and breathed
in deeply, focusing on finding all
the strength that he could muster –
the same strength that had helped
him survive countless Quests.

He tensed his muscles, ready to
act just as soon as Jeng and Kensa
made their move. He heard the
rocks around him shift and then
there was light as the last of the
rocks was removed. He jerked
upwards, ready to strike, but found
himself face-to-face with the sharp
end of Kensa's metal Lightning
Staff. Tom knew how happy she
would be to use it.

"Oh dear," Jeng said. "Who'd ever imagine seeing the Master of the Beasts laid so low? Maybe they should call you Master of Failure

instead?" Jeng gave a bark of laughter. "You didn't even survive half a day in the borderlands...and where is your little friend? Crushed like the little insect she is, I bet."

Tom gritted his teeth but made sure he kept his body very still beneath Kensa's staff. "It is you and your hopes that will be crushed. I will succeed in this Quest, and you will never get the shards."

Jeng reached down and playfully pinched Tom's cheek. "You're such an amusing little boy. It's hilarious how you always believe in yourself despite the odds stacked against you."

"Come on, Jeng, enough talking,"

Kensa snapped. She prodded Tom in the face with her staff. "Take the shard from the boy."

I need to buy time, Tom thought, his cheek throbbing where from Kensa had jabbed at him. If he could keep them talking for long enough, it would give Elenna time to come to the rescue. *If she's alive...*

Tom tried to ignore the worried voice in his head. His gaze flicked over to Jeng. "Hey, why are you really doing this? Surely, as the ruler of the kingdom, you had all the power you could ever want? Why risk your own life messing about with Beasts and Dark Magic?"

Jeng's eyes blazed. "I am the

greatest emperor to have ever lived.
Of course one kingdom isn't enough,

not when I know a whole world lies out there." His mouth twisted into a sneer. "Besides, I hear your homeland is very nice. Avantia will make a welcome addition to my empire." He shrugged. "And now that Queen Aroha of Tangala has united with King Hugo of Avantia, the defeat of one will yield two new kingdoms."

"Oh, I see! That's what this is all about." Tom rolled his eyes for extra effect. If he could just keep the emperor talking, maybe he'd have a chance.

"Excuse me?" Jeng questioned, looking confused for a moment.

Tom seized the opportunity.

"You're jealous," he explained.
"You wanted to marry Queen Aroha
yourself, but she married King Hugo
instead!"

Jeng's bald head reddened in rage
as he marched towards Tom. "How
dare you speak to me like that, you
snivelling little worm?" he yelled.

"Just kill him," said Kensa.

"With pleasure," said Jeng

With hatred twisting his lips, the
wicked emperor raised his boot
above Tom's head.

THE NEXT BEAST

"Leave him alone!"

The words echoed through the rocky valley and there was a flash of movement as Elenna charged at Jeng. With a cry of rage she shoulder-barged him out of the way, just as the emperor's boot was about to crush Tom's face.

Tom took his chance. Arching his

back, he flipped himself upwards onto his feet.

"Get back in your hole," Kensa snarled as she swung her staff. Tom sidestepped, catching it easily and then lifting Kensa up and throwing her down the stony hillside. He wasn't sure if it was the breastplate that gave him the power to do this or his joy at knowing Elenna was alive.

Tom looked over at Elenna. His friend had Jeng in a headlock. She grinned over at him. "I've got this under control. Go catch yourself a witch."

Tom nodded. There was so much he wanted to say – like how worried

he'd been about Elenna, how glad
he was that she was alive.

Elenna gave him a look that told
Tom that she knew exactly what he

was thinking. "Go," was all she said.

Tom pursued Kensa, stumbling over the uneven slope. But reaching the edge of the cliff, he saw her lying motionless at the bottom, with the staff a few paces away beside a large boulder. Tom felt a flash of concern despite himself and ran to her side. "Kensa, are you all—"

The witch suddenly kicked out and swept his feet out from beneath him. Taken by surprise, Tom landed in a heap with a thud.

"You fool!" Kensa spat, jumping up and running towards her staff.

Tom shook his head. He wouldn't make that mistake again. *Kensa only cares about herself – she doesn't deserve my sympathy.*

He sprang to his feet but the witch was already whirling the staff above her head, so fast it was little more than a blur.

Tom held his ground. He was not going to give Kensa the satisfaction of seeing him retreat.

The witch gave a high-pitched shriek as she charged, swinging the staff. Tom ducked, letting her own momentum take her to the ground. Turning on his heels, he reached for his sword, but stopped dead when the sky above him darkened, unnaturally quickly.

Tom stared up. Cloud was descending over Vareen, and the sky

seemed to pulse with crackling, fizzing bolts of lightning.

"He's coming," Kensa said. Tom looked back down and saw that the witch's face was twisted with fear. "The Beast."

And he's angry, Tom thought. He could feel it through his red jewel.

The Beast was a storm of emotion, a whirlwind of rage.

There was crackling energy in the air that made the hairs on Tom's arms prickle. *What type of Beast am I about to face?*

You shall not take it, a voice from the sky said. The sound was neither human nor animal. It was thunder and it filled Tom's head. *I am Thoron and the shard is mine to protect.*

Tom's hand trembled on the hilt of his sword. He was not this Beast's enemy, but he knew Thoron wouldn't see it like that. If Tom could just see him face-to-face then maybe he could explain that he meant no harm. But Tom couldn't see him. Thoron was obscured by a bank of dense, grey cloud.

Thoron, show yourself, Tom demanded through the jewel. *I am not your enemy. I want to keep the shard safe.*

Liar! The thundering voice rumbled and rolled around in Tom's mind and it was so loud that he felt like his head might explode. His eyes scanned the sky for some sign of the Beast, but he was still hidden behind the cloud.

You are evil trespassers, Thoron continued. *Leave now, or the next step you take into Vareen will be your last!*

Tom was about to reply when he noticed a flash of movement out of the corner of his eye. Kensa was scuttling up the hill. The witch stopped as she saw Elenna and Jeng coming down the slope. Elenna had Jeng's arms twisted up behind his back and was pushing him forward.

"Help me." Jeng's face was red with rage.

Kensa shook her head. "That girl is the least of your problems. Look!" She pointed up at the sky.

One of the clouds had split apart, revealing a trailing shape – like a swirling giant snake made of smoke. It drifted down towards the ground, its long body pulsing with light that crackled and rippled.

A pair of red eyes appeared at the head of the trail, just before a wide

mouth ripped open in the vapour
and the cloud swirled to form a
face.

Tom had never seen a Beast like it.
Thoron was made out of cloud and
had the ability to change shape!

*How can I fight a Beast I can't
touch?*

STORM OF STONE

The cloud-snake was drawing
in more thick vapour to himself,
increasing his size.

Tom took a step backwards.

*I told you to go away and yet more
of you come,* Thoron thundered.
I will end this. I will end you all.

The snake face was looking
directly at Jeng and Elenna.

Wait! Please listen to me, Tom began.

None of you belong here, the Beast said. *You must be destroyed.*

Tom swallowed, remembering that it had been a long time since any of the Beasts protecting the shards had seen people. To Thoron, every traveller was an enemy, a threat to the shard that he had sworn to safeguard. There was going to be no way to persuade him otherwise.

Tom drew his sword. He didn't want to hurt the Beast, but he also had to protect Elenna and himself.

Thoron unleashed a thunderous roar at the intruders, his whole body flashing with lightning so bright it forced Tom to his knees. Shielding his eyes with his arm, he heard the others howling in agony.

When he dared to look again, he

saw that the whole sky was a sheet of silver light as thunder boomed all around them. Like a blind beetle, Jeng was scuttling for safety behind a boulder, while Kensa remained huddled in a ball.

Tom staggered to his feet, still shielding his eyes. He felt a heavy, damp force hit his body and knock him backwards. Thoron was attacking. Tom knew the Beast's scorching flash of light might come again at any moment but he risked a glance. He then thrust out with the flat of his blade but his arm simply passed through cloud.

Thoron spat a bolt of lightning that struck the boulder where Jeng was hiding, splitting it in two and throwing the emperor backwards. He tumbled out of sight behind a row of pillars.

Thoron moved his great head to stare directly at Elenna. The Beast opened his jaws and Tom saw a white, scalding light gathering in his cavernous mouth.

"Watch out, Elenna!" Tom cried. Drawing on the power of his golden boots, he bounded towards his friend and knocked her clear of the bolt of light that ripped through the air. He threw up his shield, feeling the bolt slam into it, sending an agonising charge through the wood and snaking up his arm. The energy

lifted Tom off his feet and flung him
backwards.

He landed with a crash, his cheek
grazing painfully on the shards of
rock that studded the ground. He

lost hold of both his sword and
shield, which went skidding across
the rocky ground. He lay there for a
moment, too stunned to move. His
left arm felt completely deadened

from the lightning bolt and his head throbbed from the impact with the ground.

He bit back the groan of pain that wanted to escape from his lips. *I will not feel sorry for myself,* Tom thought. His sword and shield may have been smoking from the lightning that had hit them, but he was alive – and while there was blood in his veins, he would not give up on this Quest!

Tom staggered to his feet. Elenna was already on hers. Thoron was waiting for them, a swirling mass spiralling upwards ready to launch another attack.

Tom did not hesitate. He leapt

forwards and nimbly scooped up his sword and shield ready to do battle once more. He felt a pang of sadness as he saw how badly his shield was burnt.

But there was no time to wonder what that might mean for his shield – Thoron was descending again. The Beast's red eyes flared brightly as his body formed the shape of a massive bird, his vapoury flanks extending into wings.

With an ear-piercing screech, he swooped over Tom and Elenna, scattering bolts of lightning. For a moment, Tom thought the Beast was trying to strike them down again, but then he realised that clever

Thoron had a different plan.

The Beast was using his lightning bolts to cut deep gouges into the rocks that surrounded Tom and Elenna. A storm of deadly-sharp stone rained down on them.

Tom threw up his shield so it covered their heads as he and Elenna ran forwards. The stone fragments pounded into the wood as they raced ahead, and Tom wondered how long the shield would hold now that the wood was so badly burnt.

"Tom, we can't just keep on running," Elenna yelled over the sound of stone hitting the shield.

"I know. We need a distraction."

Tom scanned the area in front of him and then over his shoulder. "It's the only way we'll defeat Thoron and gain the next shar—"

He broke off as he saw Kensa appear on the path behind Thoron. The witch was no longer cowering in a ball. She wasn't even running in the opposite direction in an attempt to save her life. She was standing straight and tall, and wielding her metal Lightning Staff as she stealthily approached the Beast from behind.

Tom stopped running and stared in amazement at the witch. *Kensa is actually trying to help us. Maybe Thoron really can be stopped.*

A DUBIOUS BARGAIN

Tom grabbed Elenna's arm. "We've got our distraction," he told her.

Elenna had spotted Kensa as well. She nodded, but Tom saw his friend gulp as she looked up at the towering whirlwind of fury that was Thoron.

Tom took a deep breath to calm

himself. The Beast had stopped releasing lightning bolts, but was changing shape once more, his cloudy form swirling in a dark mass. There was no way to guess what type of creature Tom and Elenna would have to face next.

Tom readied his shield.

"Kensa's not trying to help us," Elenna said with a gasp. "She's trying to get the shard for herself. Look!"

Tom peered from behind his shield. Elenna was right. There, nestled in the writhing tendrils of cloud, was the icy blue shard – and now that Thoron's focus was fixed on Tom and Elenna, Kensa was taking her chance to steal it.

The witch crept closer, her hand
whipping forward as fast as a snake
as she tried to snatch the shard out
of the mass of cloud.

She came back empty-handed. It was not surprising. Thoron would not stop moving and writhing, making it hard to keep sight of the shard. Kensa's face twisted in annoyance and she raised her staff, ready to strike a mighty blow on the unknowing Beast.

"Stop!" Tom's voice echoed around the canyon. Despite the fact that Thoron was attacking them, Tom couldn't let the Beast be robbed or wounded by the Evil Witch.

Thoron let out a thundering roar in reply and surged forward out of reach of Kensa, his snarling voice filling Tom's head:

How dare you command me?

Tom hurriedly placed his fingers to his red jewel. *I was telling Kensa to stop, not you,* he replied, but he could feel that the Beast was too consumed with rage to listen.

The cloud began to swirl faster. Thoron hadn't shifted into a new shape yet. It was as if the Beast was trying to decide in what form he could wreak the most damage.

Tom spotted Kensa charging towards Thoron, staff raised, even as more lightning gathered in the belly of the Beast.

Thoron fired out another bolt. Tom swung his shield forward, deflecting the lightning at Kensa. The bolt struck her staff and made it glow a

deep red. The witch gave a squeal of
surprise as her feet left the ground.
She flailed and dropped her staff as
she was sucked up into the Beast's
body. Tom watched in awe as her
body was tossed this way and that

behind the cloud. He could see her mouth moving but the sounds of her screams were drowned out by the crackling of Thoron's lightning.

The Beast rose higher and higher in the air. *He's lost interest in me*

and Elenna now, Tom realised. *Now that he has a different intruder in his grasp.* Thoron began to drift in the direction of a rocky mountain that loomed over Vareen.

"We have to follow him," Tom said. "Whatever she's done wrong, we can't let her be killed by the Beast."

Elenna nodded. "But we still have no idea how to defeat Thoron. He doesn't have a weakness."

Tom's gaze fell to the ground, on Kensa's staff. Unlike Tom's shield the staff had not been burnt and scarred by Thoron's lightning. If anything, it seemed to radiate with energy.

Tom knelt down and looked more

closely at the staff. He'd seen the witch use this weapon to create and manipulate lightning. It could be the key to defeating Thoron... But did Tom dare to pick up such a mysterious and evil weapon?

Yes, he thought. *I must.* He grabbed the staff.

"Come on, Tom," Elenna said, looking up the mountain. "Thoron is getting away."

Tom looked up and saw the Beast disappear into a cave in the mountainside. He stood. "Then let's go!" He broke off as he heard a pained groan from behind him. Jeng had managed to crawl out from behind the stalagmites. The emperor collapsed on the ground, his chest rising and falling heavily. His eyes closed.

Tom looked at the mountain and the cave that Thoron had disappeared into. He then looked back at the emperor.

I can leave Jeng here, injured and alone, he thought. *Or I take him with me.* Tom sighed, knowing he only had one choice.

He went over to Jeng.

"What are you doing?" Elenna asked.

"We take Jeng with us," Tom explained. "That way, we can keep an eye on him."

Elenna shook her head. "He can't be trusted, Tom, and we're going to be in enough danger in that cave along with Thoron and Kensa."

"Trust me," Tom replied. He dragged Jeng up into a sitting position.

The emperor swayed there for a moment his eyes still closed. "Tell me, Kensa," Jeng whispered through dry and bloody lips. "Do we have the shard?"

"Bad luck," Tom said. "I'm not Kensa and Thoron still has the shard."

Jeng's eyes snapped open, his expression first alarmed and then vicious.

"Get your hands off me, you Avantian brat," the emperor snarled. "Will I never be rid of you?"

"I will happily go home to Avantia," Tom said calmly. "But only once I'm sure Gwildor is safe from its evil ruler!"

Elenna sniffed. "You don't need to worry, Tom. Jeng won't be ruler for much longer."

The emperor smirked and got to

his feet, still a little unsteady. "Then you don't know my kingdom very well. Word doesn't travel all that fast around here. There will still be vast swathes of Gwildor where nobody has heard about what happened in the capital – which means there are still many, many people who remain loyal to me."

"Not for long," Tom promised. He nodded his head in the direction of the mountain. "You're coming with us to Thoron's cave – your partner-in-crime has got herself into a bit of trouble."

"I will not be ordered about by a mere boy," the emperor spluttered.

"Yes, you will," Elenna said,

pointing an arrow at him.

"Fine," Jeng growled, "but only because having you two fools at my side might make it a little bit easier for me to get my hands on the shard."

Elenna raised an eyebrow. "Carry on dreaming," she said. "Now walk."

They walked in silence across the rocky valley and finally the cave's entrance was just a few steps away. Tom looked into the darkness. "Time to go in."

He hoped he sounded more confident than he felt. The idea of going into the vast cave sent a chill down his spine. They were going into the unknown to face a Beast unlike no other. Tom didn't know if he'd ever see daylight again.

"Are you sure this is a good idea?" Jeng's voice trembled as he stared into the darkness.

"Of course it is," Elenna said. "Keep walking."

Jeng shuffled a few paces ahead of them. Elenna had her arrow trained on his back, but Tom could see that his friend looked worried too. "What is it?" he whispered.

Elenna's pursed her lips in a thin line. "This cave is full of dangers and Jeng is one of the most crafty cowards I've ever encountered," she murmured. "The idea of him in a cave with us really doesn't appeal to me..."

"It will be all right," Tom assured her. "I'll make sure of that."

THE BELLY OF THE BEAST

"I think Jeng should go first," Elenna said as they reached the threshold. She gave the emperor a rough shove in the back. "Please, 'Your Majesty', lead the way," she added sarcastically.

Inside, the cave was hot and damp and Tom could see flashes of light at the end of one of the tunnels. *Is it Thoron's lightning?* he wondered. He didn't know – but what choice did they have other than to hope that the light led to the Beast?

The cave was filled with the sound of their footsteps on the rocky path,

and the steady drip of water from far away – there was no sound of whirling wind or thunder.

"Are you even sure Thoron's in here?" asked Jeng.

"We saw him go in," Elenna hissed. "Keep on walking."

"Doesn't mean he's still here, though," Jeng muttered. "Maybe he's already left."

Tom hated to admit it, but Jeng was right. They needed a way to check. Surely Kensa was running out of time.

"Use your red jewel," Elenna suggested.

Tom nodded and closed his eyes for a moment, drawing on the power of the red stone. All of a sudden, his head was filled with Thoron's thundering thoughts:

People are not to be trusted. Wherever they tread, they bring only destruction...

"He's here," Tom said. "And he's not feeling very welcoming."

They carried on, the path twisting and turning as they ventured further into the cave. Eventually, it spat them out of the tunnel and into a wide cavern with a low, rocky ceiling.

In front of them, Tom could see the Beast floating, suspended, with Kensa still tumbling around inside him. She was completely limp and her eyes were closed.

Tom felt a tremor of unease. He needed to show Thoron that he was worthy of the shard, and he could only do that by beating him in combat. His hand tightened on Kensa's staff. *How can I defeat a Beast that is made of cloud and can change into any shape he wants? How can I fight with a magical weapon I've never wielded before?*

There was only one way to find out. It was time to go into battle.

He turned to Elenna. "Keep an eye on Jeng for me, will you?"

"You shouldn't fight Thoron alone," Elenna protested. "I should help you."

"You will be as long as you don't let Jeng get in the way."

Elenna nodded, but looked frustrated.

Tom strode forward, holding the Lightning Staff in both hands.

You dare come into my cave, Thoron roared in Tom's head. He fired out a lashing whip of white hot energy. Tom did not hesitate. He raised the staff, the metal rod cold in his hand, and met the lightning bolt with Kensa's weapon. The energy travelled along the staff and made it glow. Tom felt the whole weapon shudder and get hot. He expected pain but he felt only... power. Even the aches and pains he

had picked up from being buried
under the rocks earlier that day
faded, as if healing themselves.

Tom marvelled at the staff in his
hand. Somehow it had absorbed

the lightning's energy!

Thoron gave a rumbling roar of frustration and began to shapeshift. Two columns emerged from the cloud Beast and Tom realised they were giant legs. The Beast's enormous feet planted themselves firmly on the ground as powerful arms thrust out of the whirlwind and then a head huge appeared out of the swirl.

Thoron is taking on some kind of human shape, Tom realised.

"Who is he changing into?" Elenna cried from behind, her voice almost lost under the rumbling roar.

"I don't know," Tom said, staring up at Thoron.

"I think I do," Jeng said. "Look closely."

Tom did, and realised that the cloud-Beast's face was familiar. It was Kensa.

Thoron was moulding around the witch's form, creating a giant version of her, made of vapour and lightning. The Beast charged at Tom, arms outstretched as if to strangle him.

Tom ducked down and jabbed out with the staff, the jagged end opening up a wound in Thoron's human-like flank.

With a thud, Kensa fell free of the Beast through the wound, and rolled across the floor. Elenna leapt

forward, grabbed the witch's arm
and dragged her to safety.

The Beast gave a roar of rage and
turned himself into a cloud-swirl
once more. Even in this form Tom
could still see the injury that he'd
inflicted on Thoron. The blue shard

of the Broken Star which spun around inside the cloud had been dragged close to it. *If I get close enough, I'll be able to reach in and grab the next shard,* Tom thought.

He barrelled forward, dropping the staff to the ground and thrusting one hand into the Beast's swirling mass. His fingers grazed the shard. It felt cool and smooth to the touch. He pushed in further, trying to get a proper grip on it but felt Thoron's heavy, damp fingers clamp around his waist, and then his feet left the floor.

As Tom was raised up, he saw a huge, yawning mouth appear in the heart of the swirling whirlwind.

He tried to fight his way free, but there was nothing he could do. The Beast swallowed him whole, the thick cloud clogging up Tom's nose and mouth, making it impossible to draw enough air into his lungs.

Tom fell downwards, tumbling through lightning-streaked cloud. And then he wasn't falling any longer. He was held in place, suspended in mid-air.

It was quiet in the centre of the Beast. The sound of thunder was completely gone, almost as if he was underwater. Tom spotted the shard just out of arm's reach and he kicked forwards to try and grab it.

But as he moved, he felt himself

somersault in the air and then continue to flip over again and again, just like Kensa had done when she had been trapped inside Thoron.

Blood rushed to his head, dizziness sweeping through him.

I'm too tired to fight, Tom realised. *I'm too tired to escape... This is the end.*

FROZEN!

"Tom, wake up! Tom!"

The silence inside the Beast was broken, with a muffled, distant voice. It was Elenna screaming his name.

He tried to focus. Staring through the swirling mass of cloud, he could see his friend running forward, leaving Kensa and Jeng behind. She was now standing right next to the Beast. Too close. Tom tried to keep his eyes open. He wanted to warn his friend but his voice came out as barely a croak.

"Don't you dare pass out," Elenna yelled. She ducked as the Beast lashed out at her. "Thoron has taken your form. How am I supposed to fight a Tom-shaped Beast?"

Tom's eyes snapped open, anger flashing through him. *The Beast has taken on my shape. And now he is attacking my best friend.*

He was still spinning in a circle and the dizziness was getting worse, but he could not let himself surrender to unconsciousness.

He felt the thud of heavy footsteps
vibrate around him as Thoron

strode forward. Through the cloud, Tom saw Elenna pick up the Lightning Staff and bravely stand in Thoron's way while Jeng and Kensa cowered behind her.

The air around Tom was heavy with static electricity and the streaks of lightning that studded the Beast's cloudy form were glowing brighter. Thoron was about to release a lightning bolt.

"You can defeat the Beast," Tom called out to Elenna. "I believe in you."

He wasn't sure if Elenna heard him but his friend bravely blocked the first lightning blast from Thoron's fingers with the staff, staggering backwards.

"Ha! Is that your best shot?" she cried.

Tom could tell that she was trying to get Thoron to lose his temper and let down his guard. His friend struck out with the staff but the Beast leapt back, avoiding the jagged end. Tom could sense Thoron's nervousness, his cloudy form fading to a mud-like colour. Elenna was strong and getting stronger from the power she was absorbing from the staff.

"Go on, Elenna, you can do it," Tom cried.

His friend moved forward to strike again when Tom saw it – a rock hurtling in Elenna's direction.

"Elenna, watch out!" he shouted.
But it was too late. The heavy rock
hit her shoulder and she slumped to

the ground with a cry of pain and let go of the staff. Tom saw Jeng looking smug as he dusted off his hands.

That treacherous, evil...

Tom didn't get to finish his thought. From inside Thoron, he felt the lightning charge building for a killing blast. With a roar, the Beast surged towards where Elenna lay, prone and defenceless.

There's no time, Tom thought, desperately. *I wish I could stop things for just a moment so that I can think...*

And perhaps there was a way he could! He remembered the white shard that was still hanging from his belt. The shard could create an icy blast in an instant – an icy blast that might just stop Thoron in his tracks.

The speed of his spinning continued to increase but Tom gritted his teeth, reached for his belt and plucked the shard from the pouch. Thoron stood above Elenna. Through the red jewel, Tom sensed the Beast's murderous rage. He closed his fist around the cold star fragment, letting his fear and adrenaline flow through into it.

Thoron raised a huge fist, ready to smash Elenna out of existence.

As Tom clutched the shard, freezing cold air flowed from the

fragment and pulsed all around
him in cool blue waves. Tom could
see the cloud solidifying, frosty
icicles studding the air until he
was completely surrounded by ice.
Thoron was being frozen from the
inside. Straining against the cold
currents, he was trying to bring
down his fist, but he couldn't. With
a cry, Tom summoned the power of
his golden breastplate, pushing his
fist forward and punching his way
free of his ice prison.

Tom tumbled to the ground next
to Elenna, the sounds that filled
the cave rushing to his ears. They
both leapt to their feet and turned
round to face the Beast. Tom put

away the white shard and drew his
sword, prepared to fight. Elenna
had readied her bow and arrow. But
Thoron was frozen in place, still in
the shape of Tom, his mouth open in
a silent roar.

The Beast's red eyes glinted
brightly, but Tom sensed no anger.

Thoron's voice filled his head.

You have defeated me, Son of Gwildor, the Beast said. *My shard is yours.*

Tom looked down and saw the shard emerging from the frozen belly of the Beast. He reached out for it.

"Now!" Jeng suddenly shouted.

Tom spun round to see both the emperor and the witch lunge forward to grab the second shard. He easily dodged Jeng and stepped behind him, bringing his blade up to the villain's throat.

But Kensa had managed to grab her staff, which she was now pointing at Elenna's head.

"Looks like it is a stalemate," Tom said, wishing that Thoron wasn't still frozen and could come to their aid now that he had realised Tom wasn't his enemy. "I guess we should both drop our weapons."

Kensa laughed. "I don't think so."

"Drop it or Jeng gets hurt," Tom

promised grimly. "I'm not bluffing."

Kensa shrugged. "Thing is, I'm willing to gamble that you are – and even if you're not, you care a lot more about the girl than I do about Jeng." She nodded her head at the emperor. "Let him go, or she dies."

"Um…maybe we should talk about this?" said Jeng.

Elenna's face was composed as she looked at Tom. "Don't listen to her. The Quest is more important than me."

Tom shook his head. He could see from the evil glint in Kensa's eyes that the witch was serious. She'd end Elenna's life in a heartbeat. With a growl of frustration, he dropped his blade from Jeng's throat and the emperor scuttled to one of the caverns.

"Good, good," said Kensa. "Now hand over the white shard first, and

then the blue one. Nice and slowly, now – there's a good boy."

Tom nodded and tried to ignore the furious look on Elenna's face. He had no choice. Not if he wanted to save his best friend's life.

He got ready to release the white shard from his belt when Elenna quickly threw a punch into Kensa's face. The witch gave a yelp of surprise, lowering her staff and holding her bleeding nose. Elenna then stepped forwards, swinging her leg out to trip Kensa up.

As Elenna darted across the cave floor towards Tom, Kensa was scrambling to her feet, swinging the staff to fire a lightning bolt after her.

But the witch's aim was hasty and clumsy, and the lightning hit the roof of the cavern. Fragments of rock started to rain down – jagged chunks hitting the ground with bone-shaking thuds.

"Jeng, quick!" Kensa called. "We need to leave before the whole roof comes down. There are still two shards unclaimed. Victory will be ours."

The villains fled the cave. More than anything, Tom wanted to chase them. It was his duty to bring them to justice once and for all, but he needed to do something about the rockfall first. His fingers went to the white shard that hung from his belt. He had an idea.

Using the star fragment, he sent a bolt of icy air up to the ceiling of the cave. Ice crept across the surface freezing the falling rocks in place.

"Nice work," Elenna said, looking up at the dangling icicles.

"Nice jab," Tom replied.

Elenna grinned. "I look forward to doing it again when we catch up with those cowards."

Tom turned to face the Beast and saw that Thoron's human form was slowly beginning to melt, and reshape itself into a swirling cloud with red eyes.

You are a true hero, the Beast's thundery voice sounded in

Tom's head. *You are the hero that this kingdom needs.*

The second shard dropped to the cave floor, and Elenna picked it up.

Listen carefully, Tom, Thoron continued. *Gwildor's fate is in your hands. You must not fail.*

I will not, Tom promised.

Elenna came to stand at his side and handed him the blue shard. Now that Tom had two fragments of the Broken Star in his grasp, he felt a powerful, magnetic pull between the pieces.

"They're trying to join together!" he said to Elenna.

"Irina said they would form a powerful weapon when combined,"

replied his friend.

Tom decided to keep them apart for now. If the Good Witch was right, the weapon might be difficult to control.

Perhaps there will be a time when I need the unpredictable power of such an incredible weapon, Tom thought. But for now, I know Thoron's shard will be required for my next Quest.

He turned to leave the cavern behind, trying to ignore the dread that sat heavy in his chest. "Come on," he said. "Our work in Gwildor is far from finished..."

CONGRATULATIONS, YOU HAVE COMPLETED THIS QUEST!

At the end of each chapter you were awarded a special gold coin.
The QUEST in this book was worth an amazing 8 coins.

Look at the Beast Quest totem picture inside the back cover of this book to see how far you've come in your journey to become

MASTER OF THE BEASTS.

The more books you read, the more coins you will collect!

Do you want your own Beast Quest Totem?

1. Cut out and collect the coin below
2. Go to the Beast Quest website
3. Download and print out your totem
4. Add your coin to the totem
www.beastquest.co.uk/totem

Don't miss the next exciting Beast Quest book, OKKO THE SAND MONSTER!

Read on for a sneak peek...

KENSA'S PORTAL

Tom blinked as he emerged from the cave, his eyes taking a few moments to adjust. Bright light reflected off the snowy mountains that soared a thousand feet into the clouds. Tom turned to see Elenna following him out of the cave, rubbing her side. She slumped down on a rock.

"Are you hurt?" Tom asked.
He knew the fight against Thoron
had been bruising for both of them.

"Nothing that a good long rest
wouldn't fix," Elenna replied with a
rueful grin.

"I wish we could rest," Tom said.
"But we must follow Kensa and Jeng.
They can't have got far, and if they
get their hands on the third fragment
of the Broken Star, they could cause
untold havoc."

Tom felt guilty about pushing
his friend to go on, but they simply
couldn't stop now. The wicked
sorceress Kensa, along with the
treacherous Emperor Jeng of

Gwildor, had fled North, to the rarely visited areas of the kingdom. They sought the four fragments of a fallen comet, known as the Broken Star. Each fragment in isolation had powers that could control the weather – the four combined were thought to be an unstoppable force.

Many years before, to stop the fragments falling into the wrong hands, the Good Witch Clara had placed each fragment with a Good Beast under the instructions to protect them at all costs.

"Don't worry," Elenna said, getting to her feet. "I'm ready for anything."

Tom grinned at her. He knew she wouldn't let him down. Turning, he scanned the craggy mountains surrounding them. Thanks to the power of his golden helmet, Tom's eyesight was sharper than an eagle's.

He saw no sign of their enemies. The area around Vareen was utterly barren. Not a blade of grass broke the landscape. No birds flew, no insects crawled over the rocks. He was about to give up, when...

Wait!

In a deep valley between two distant mountains he saw a telltale flicker of colour and movement amidst the drab colours. "There!" he cried. Now he knew where to look, he focussed on the two villains. Kensa was unmistakeable in her

black cloak. Jeng, in his flowing
robes, walked a few feet behind,
stumbling and clearly tired.

"So what are we waiting for?"
Elenna asked, her voice grim. "Let's
get after them."

They jogged side by side, taking a higher route above the valley. Tom felt blisters forming on his feet, but he knew he couldn't stop. They were gaining on their prey.

"Careful," Elenna panted as Tom sped up, scattering dust and pebbles down the slope. "The stones are unstable."

"We can't let them get away," Tom replied. "They deserve to be in a jail cell, along with their friend, Sanpao the pirate."

"You're not going to be putting anyone in a jail cell if you tumble off the side of this mountain," Elenna pointed out. Even as she said this, Tom's ankle turned on a loose stone.

He felt his stomach lurch as he swayed perilously close to the edge of the ridge and the plummeting drop to the knife-sharp rocks below. Elenna was right. He slowed his pace a little, picking his way more carefully through the treacherous rocks.

Turning his attention to Kensa and Jeng again, Tom saw that the pair had stopped at a high, sheer rock face. Kensa seemed to be inspecting it carefully. Tom saw Jeng lower himself onto a reddish rock, his shoulders slumping in exhaustion. Tom and Elenna crept closer.

"What are they doing?" Elenna whispered.

"I don't know," Tom replied. "But they've walked into a dead end. We should strike now, while they're trapped."

"They'll hear us coming," Elenna warned. "Kensa will use her Lightning Staff against us."

As she spoke, Tom saw Kensa reach into her cloak and pull out a glass vial. They watched the witch dip her finger into the container like it was an inkwell and draw something on the cliff face.

A five-pointed star.

A brilliant flash of light lit the sombre scene and they watched Jeng slide off the rock, cowering behind it as the rock face began to shimmer.

"A portal!" Tom cried. "Quick,
they'll get away! We have to go now!"

They scrambled down the slope as
fast as they could. As he ran, Tom

saw Kensa and Jeng pass through the glowing portal, disappearing in an instant. Immediately, the portal began to shrink. Tom sprinted harder, clattering over loose rocks despite the risk. *We have to follow them through.*

"Run, Elenna!" he cried. They were twenty paces away, now ten, but the portal had nearly closed. They weren't going to make it. Unless…

Read *Okko the Sand Monster* to find out what happens next!

Discover the new Beast Quest mobile game from

Available free on iOS and Android

Guide Tom on his Quest to free the Good Beasts
of Avantia from Malvel's evil spells.

Battle the Beasts, defeat the minions,
unearth the secrets and collect
rewards as you journey through the
Kingdom of Avantia.

DOWNLOAD THE APP TO BEGIN
THE ADVENTURE NOW!